created by: BJ Hendricks & Robert J Mulligan III

created by: BJ Hendricks & Robert J Mulligan III

artwork by: Dinh "Monstrous" Nguyen

presented by: George Cameron Romero

published by: IbbiLane Press

A is for Ava,
with guts on the lawn.

B is for Brian,
Who's head is now gone.

C is for Cameron
Who was clawed in the face.

D is for Dave
While walking in place.

E is for Emily,
who has now lost her leg.

F is for Faith,
being shared with a pig.

G is for Gina,
who died playing fiddle.

H is for Hannah, who was split down the middle.

I is for Ian,
killed while enjoying
his habit.

J is for Jason,
being shared with a rabbit.

K is for Kelly,
who died very slow.

L is for Lloyd,
who took her photo.

M is for Michael,
who died singing a song.

N is for Nick,
who's arms are all gone.

O is for Owen,
and his missing hands.

P is for Peter,
who's dead in the sand.

Q is for Quinn
who bleeds from the mouth.

R is for Rob,
who's neck was ripped out.

S is for Sarah,
eaten down to the knees.

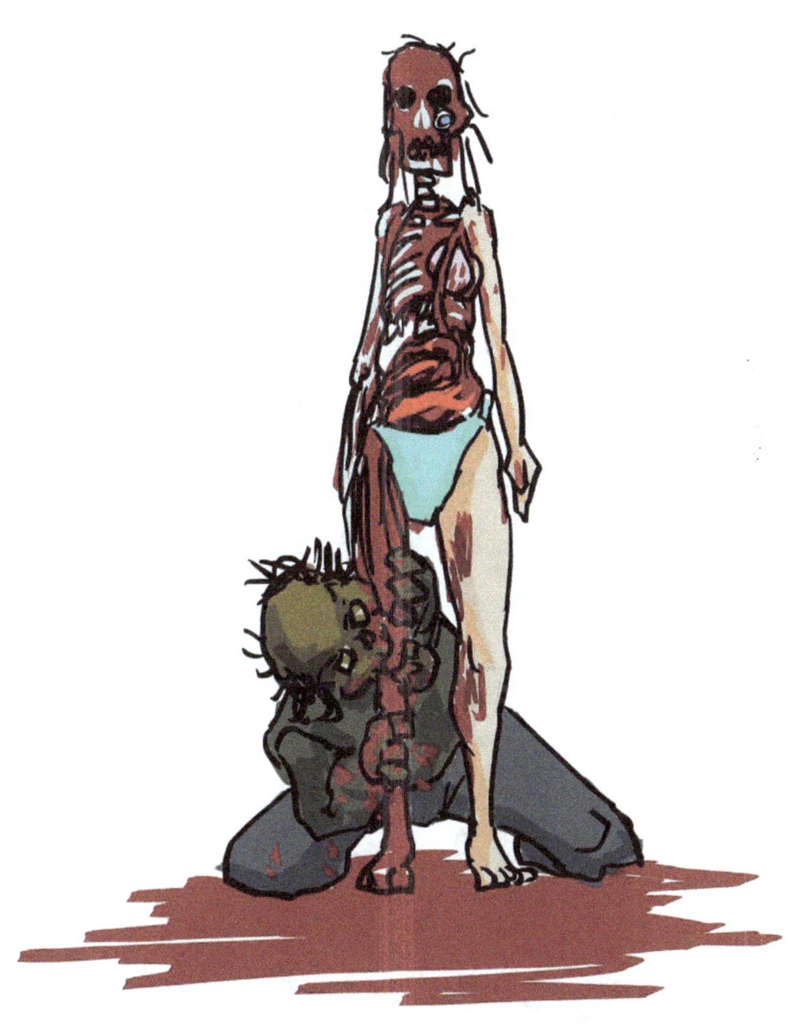

T is for Tim,
disemboweled from a tree.

U is for Uma,
whose heart is a steal.

V is for Val,
the sexiest meal.

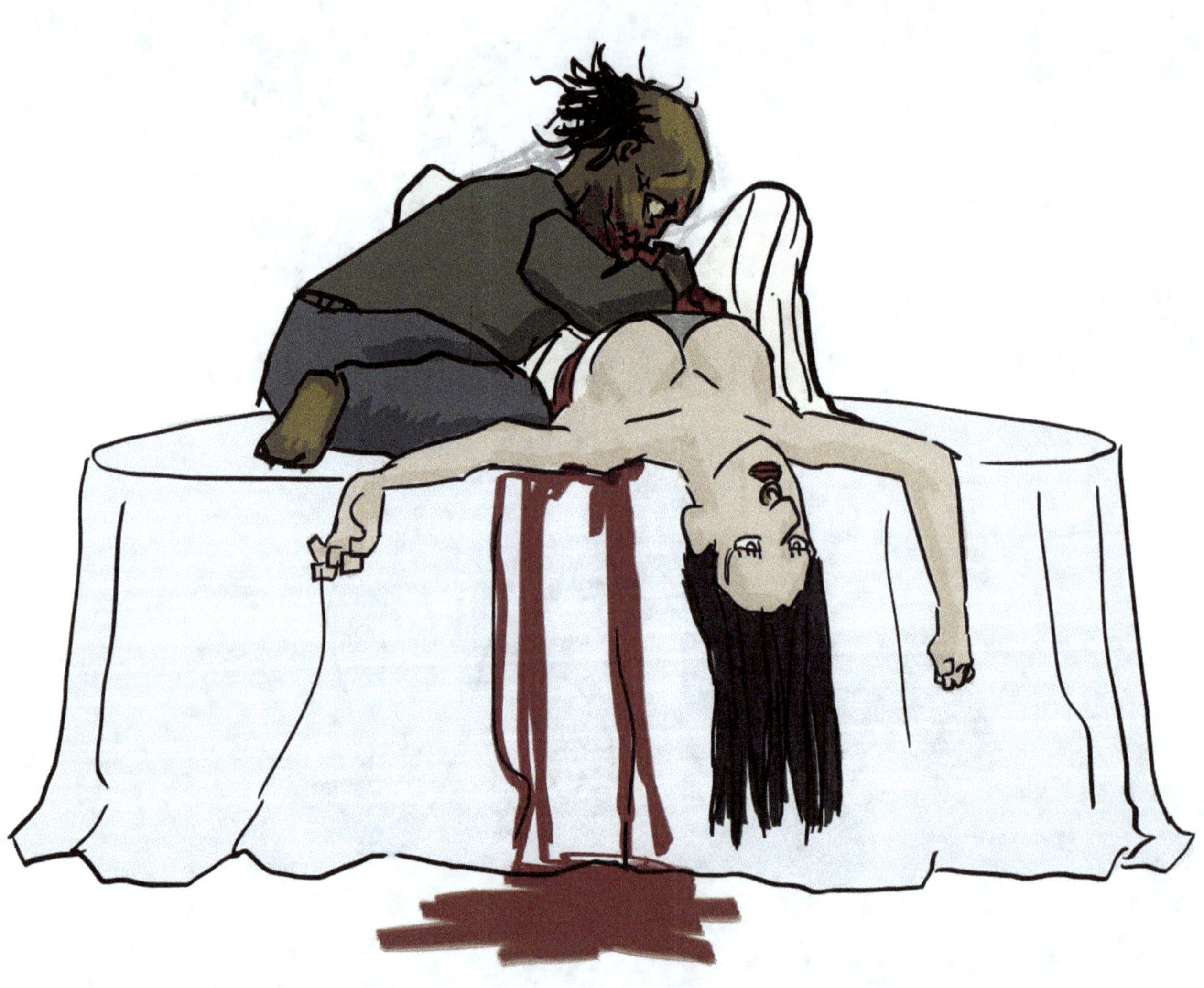

W is for Willie,
too stoned to even care.

X is for Xavier,
who was shared with a bear.

Y is for YOU,
soon to be rotten,
dead and smelly.
YOUR NAME HERE

If it wasn't for the ZOMBIE already having a full belly!!!!!!

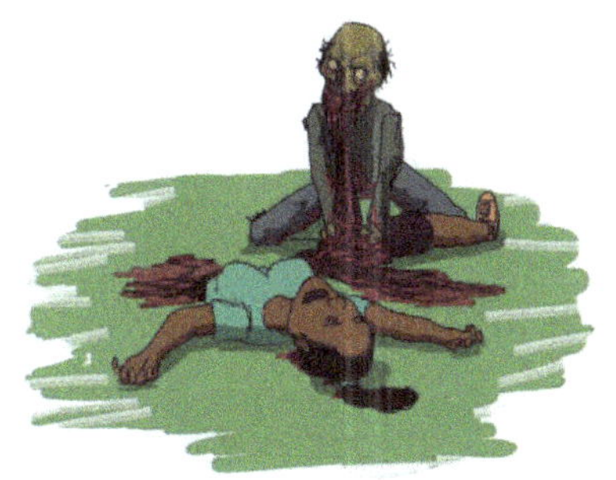
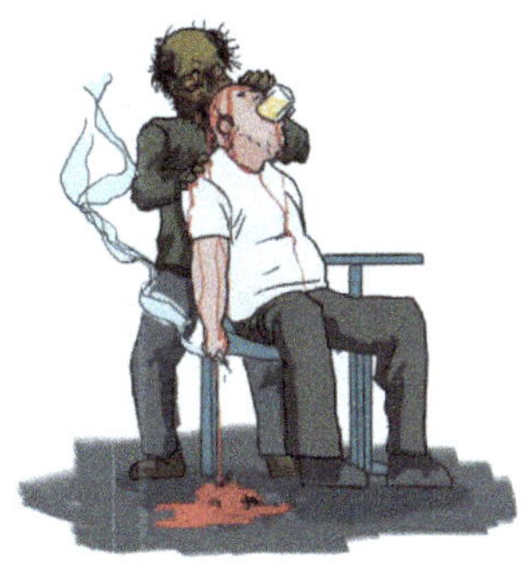

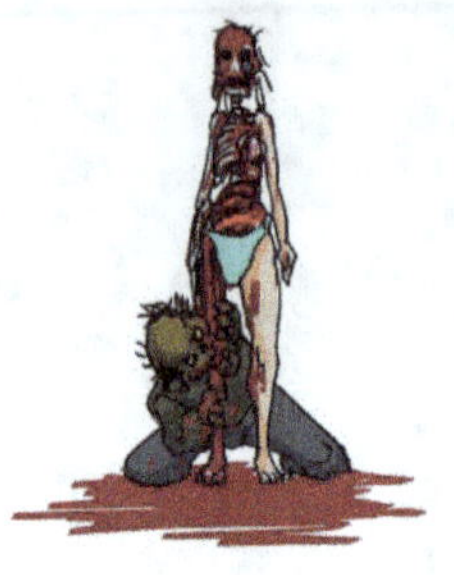

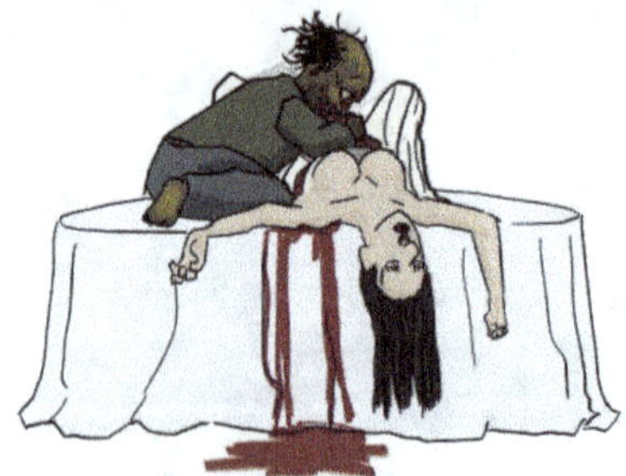

Y is for YOU,
soon to be rotten,
dead and smelly.

www.ingramcontent.com/pod-product-compliance
Lightning Source LLC
Chambersburg PA
CBHW081127300726
48982CB00005B/870

* 9 7 8 0 6 9 2 8 3 8 6 3 1 *